Ursula and her cousins stared at one another for a moment.

'Let's play Cowboys and Indians,' said Ian, a gleam in his eye. 'Ursula and that stupid teddy can be the Cowboys.'

Ursula was surprised. Every time they had played Cowboys and Indians before, Ursula always had to be the Indian, because everybody knew that Cowboys always won.

But, if Ursula's horrible, teasing cousins have a surprise for her, she has a surprise for them too. Whenever she wants to, Ursula can turn herself into a real, live little bear!

Also available:
URSULA SAILING

BY MYSELF books are specially selected to
be suitable for beginner readers.
Other BY MYSELF books available from
Young Corgi Books include:

Ursula Camping

Sheila Lavelle

Illustrated by Thelma Lambert

YOUNG CORGI BOOKS

URSULA CAMPING

A YOUNG CORGI BOOK 0 552 524476

Originally published in Great Britain in 1986 by
Hamish Hamilton Children's Books

PRINTING HISTORY
Young Corgi edition published 1987
Reprinted 1987 (twice)

This book is set in 14/18 pt Garamond 49 Medium
by Colset Private Limited, Singapore.

Corgi Books are published by Transworld
Publishers Ltd., 61–63 Uxbridge Road, Ealing,
London W5 5SA, in Australia by Transworld
Publishers (Aust.) Pty. Ltd., 15–23 Helles Avenue,
Moorebank, NSW 2170, and in New Zealand by
Transworld Publishers (N.Z.) Ltd., Cnr. Moselle and
Waipareira Avenues, Henderson, Auckland.

Printed and bound in Great Britain by
Cox & Wyman Ltd., Reading, Berks.

Ursula Camping

Chapter One

Fredbear was an old teddy with hardly any fur left at all. His stuffing was coming out at the seams and he only had one eye, but Ursula loved him better than anything else in the world.

Ursula's Aunt Prudence had once put Fredbear in the dustbin, and the dustcart

had very nearly taken him away. Luckily
Ursula got him out just in time, all covered
in tea-leaves and orange peel.

Aunt Prudence knew that Ursula loved
bears, but Ursula had a very special secret
that her aunt didn't know. The secret was a
magic spell.

Ursula had found the spell in a book in the library. It said that a little girl could turn herself into a real, live bear by eating a currant bun, stuffed with a mixture of porridge oats and honey.

Ursula had never heard of such a thing, but she tried the spell and found that it

really worked. Now she could turn into a bear whenever she liked, and a plate of beefburgers and chips would quickly turn her back into herself again.

One sunny morning Ursula was sitting on a rug in the garden with Fredbear in her

lap. She was telling him a story about a brave teddy who sailed around the world, and Fredbear was listening hard with his one good ear.

Aunt Prudence came into the garden, reading a letter the postman had just put into the letterbox.

'How would you like to have a holiday in the New Forest, Ursula?' she said. 'Your Aunt Maggie has invited us for a few days.'

'Are there bears in the New Forest?' asked Ursula hopefully, but Aunt Prudence smiled and shook her head.

'Not any more,' she said. 'But we can take Fredbear with us. And there'll be Ian and Jamie for you to play with.'

Ursula made a face. Her two cousins Ian and Jamie were rude and noisy and hated girls. Last time Ursula stayed with them they had tied her to a tree and left her there all tea-time. Ursula had missed fish and chips and chocolate pudding, and had got

a good telling-off as well. She didn't say what had really happened because she never told tales.

'Ian and Jamie are horrible,' she scowled. 'They get me into trouble all the time.'

Aunt Prudence laughed.

'They're bigger now,' she said. 'Perhaps they've learnt some manners.' She looked again at the letter in her hand. 'Aunt Maggie says if the weather stays fine you can camp out in the woods.'

Ursula's eyes shone.

'You mean sleep in a tent?' she said, jumping up and down on the lawn and sending Fredbear tumbling into the flower-bed. 'A real tent? With a real camp-stove for cooking sausages?'

'Yes, I expect so,' smiled Aunt Prudence.

Ursula went to pack her bag.

Chapter Two

On Saturday morning Ursula and Aunt
Prudence and Fredbear took the train to
Lyndhurst. Fredbear sat on Ursula's knee
all the way, looking out of the window at
the fields and the trees and the black and
white cows.

Aunt Maggie was waiting for them at

the station with Ian and Jamie. The two boys hooted with laughter when they saw Ursula.

'Cor! What a baby!' said Ian. 'Look, Jamie. She's brought her teddy!'

'Well, she's only a girl,' sneered Jamie. 'What else can you expect?'

'And it's the tattiest teddy I've ever seen,' said Ian, prodding Fredbear's bald tummy. The two boys began to dance about on the platform, singing 'Tatty old teddy! Tatty old teddy!' at the tops of their voices.

Ursula scowled and put out her tongue. Aunt Maggie kissed Ursula's cheek and smiled at her.

'Take no notice, Ursula,' she said. 'Come along, boys. Carry some of these bags to the car.'

In the car it was worse. Ursula had to sit

in the back between her two cousins, who had a lot of fun throwing Fredbear back and forth over Ursula's head. Aunt Prudence and Aunt Maggie were so busy chatting

they didn't even notice, and Ursula could do nothing except grit her teeth and wish she had never come.

Uncle Andy was taking a chicken pie out of the oven when they reached the house. Ursula loved her Uncle Andy. He was fat and cuddly and cheerful, and he was the best cook in the world.

'Chicken pie and chips, with strawberries and ice-cream to follow,' he said. Ursula hugged him tight. He had cooked her favourite lunch, and it made her feel better already.

Ian and Jamie didn't dare tease Ursula when their father was there, and after lunch they all went out into the garden.

The house was right on the edge of the forest, with no fence between, so that you couldn't tell where the garden ended and the forest began. The boys often camped out at night in the summer, and Uncle Andy had taught them the proper way to look after a camp-stove so that it was quite safe.

It didn't take long to put up the tents in two small clearings among the trees.

'Ian and Jamie can share this one,' said Uncle Andy, spreading sleeping bags and thick furry rugs on the ground. 'Ursula can have the smaller one nearer the house. You're sure you won't be frightened, Ursula, sleeping out here in the dark?'

'I'll be all right,' said Ursula, who couldn't wait to sleep in a real tent for the first time in her life. 'Fredbear will keep me company.'

Ian and Jamie sniggered and nudged one another. Ursula made sure Uncle Andy wasn't looking. Then she kicked them both hard on the shin.

Chapter Three

Uncle Andy promised to come back at tea-
time to bring the food and to help with the
stove.

'No fighting, do you hear?' he said to
the boys. 'And no teasing your cousin.'
Then he went back to the house.

Ursula and her cousins stared at one

another for a moment.

'Let's play Cowboys and Indians,' said Ian, a gleam in his eye. 'Ursula and that stupid teddy can be the Cowboys.'

Ursula was surprised. Every time they had played Cowboys and Indians before, Ursula always had to be the Indian, because everybody knew that the Cowboys always won. She wondered what her cousin was up to.

'Come on, Jamie,' said Ian. 'We'll get dressed up. Your tent is the Cowboys' camp, Ursula. You and Fredbear have to wait there for the Indians to attack.' And off went the two boys into the forest.

Ursula didn't much like the idea of waiting to be attacked. She made herself a rifle out of a long stick, and a smaller one for Fredbear. Then she lay on her stomach in the opening of her tent, listening to the birds singing. It was so peaceful that she almost fell asleep.

Suddenly the peace was shattered by ear-splitting whoops and yells. Two Indians with painted faces and feathers in their hair charged into Ursula's clearing.

She aimed her rifle at once.

'Bang! Bang! You're both dead!' she shouted gleefully. 'I shot you both!'

The Indians only laughed.

'You missed,' they said. 'You're a rotten shot. You're only a girl.'

They danced wildly round the tent, screaming and howling and waving their bows and arrows. Then, before Ursula could stop them, they snatched Fredbear from her side and ran off into the woods.

Ursula threw away her wooden rifle in disgust.

'I might have known they'd cheat,' she said to herself gloomily.

Making as little noise as possible, Ursula crept through the trees towards the boys' camp. She could hear them giggling and

talking as she drew nearer, and she hid
among some ferns to find out what was
going on.

'We'll wait until dark,' Ian was saying.
'Then we'll light the fire. We'll burn our
prisoner at the stake.'

Ursula parted the leaves with her hands and peered through into the clearing. And what she saw made her eyes grow rounder and rounder.

Ian and Jamie had made a totem-pole out of a branch of a tree and stuck it into the ground. They had decorated it with painted symbols and fierce-looking masks, and were now busy piling dry leaves and twigs round the bottom of it to make a fire. Roped tightly to the totem-pole, his head hanging limply forward on his chest, was Fredbear.

Chapter Four

Uncle Andy was surprised to see Ursula at the back door.

'I'm just bringing the stuff for your tea,' he said, filling a picnic hamper with sausages and baked beans and cherry cake and lemonade. 'Are you having a good time?'

'Great,' said Ursula. 'We're playing

Cowboys and Indians. Me and Fredbear are the Cowboys.'

She put her arms round her uncle's large waist. 'Will you make me a special Cowboy bun?' she pleaded. 'It has to have honey and porridge in the middle.'

Ursula smiled at her uncle hopefully. If this plan worked, she could teach those boys a lesson they would never forget.

Uncle Andy laughed so much all his chins wobbled.

'One special cowboy bun coming up,' he said, opening the bread bin. 'Anything else you'd like? Any other special Cowboy food?'

'Have you got any beefburgers?' breathed Ursula. 'And a few chips?'

Her uncle laughed even harder.

'You must be a very modern sort of

Cowboy,' he grinned, shaking his head. But he put the frying pan on the stove, and Ursula sighed in relief. Now she would have everything she needed for her plan to work.

Uncle Andy carried the hamper down the garden into the woods. While he was lighting the small camp-stove in the clearing near her tent, Ursula hid the currant bun and the beefburgers and chips in her sleeping bag.

The smell of frying sausages brought the two Indians running out of the trees.

'Why didn't you bring Fredbear?' asked Ursula.

'He's a bit tied up at the moment,' giggled Ian, winking at his brother. And Jamie almost choked on his lemonade.

Uncle Andy made sure they had everything they needed and that the sausages were cooking nicely.

'You can take over now, kids,' he said.
'Put yourselves to bed when it gets dark.
I'll pop down later to make sure you're all

right.' He went back to the house.

The food tasted wonderful in the open air and Ursula was hungry, but she managed to stop herself from eating too much. She had a lot more eating to do before the night was over.

The boys put out the stove and packed everything neatly back in the hamper when they had all finished. It began to grow dark.

'Come on, Jamie,' said Ian suddenly. 'Let's go.' He picked up his father's matches from beside the stove and together they slipped away through the trees.

Chapter Five

As soon as the boys had gone Ursula dived into her tent and burrowed down the sleeping bag until she found the special currant bun.

'I'M A BEAR, I'M A BEAR, I'M A BEAR,' she chanted, taking large bites and chewing as fast as she could. 'I'M A BEAR,

I'M A BEAR, I'M A BEAR.'

A few minutes later, a tawny owl hunting for his supper almost crashed into a tree in surprise. A brown furry creature, with round ears and black shining eyes, was capering madly about in the clearing. It was Ursula. Once again the magic had done its work, and Ursula had turned into a bear.

Ursula scampered off into the forest. There was no time to waste if she was going to save her precious Fredbear. Even now

those wicked cousins of hers could be lighting the fire beneath him.

She reached the boys' camp at last and
hid behind a tree to get her breath back.

Loud yells and shrieks made her peer
anxiously forward through the gloom.

The Indians were performing a wild
war-dance round and round the totem-

pole, stamping their feet and waving wooden tomahawks in the air. Fredbear still hung forlornly from the pole, bits of his stuffing poking out through the worn fur.

Ursula clenched her paws fiercely when she saw Ian approach the totem-pole, the box of matches in his hand. He opened the box, took out a match and struck it. He was holding the flame out towards the bonfire when Ursula hurled herself at him out of the forest.

The match fell harmlessly into the grass and went out. Ian cried out in fright as the strange wild beast attacked him, roaring and growling and snapping at his ankles with sharp little teeth.

Jamie didn't stay to help his brother. He fled towards the house, bumping into trees

in his haste, and shouting for his father as
he went.

Ursula left Ian and ran after Jamie. She
flung her paws round his legs like a rugby
player on the television and brought him

crashing to the ground. Then she growled
in his ear and waved her claws in his face.

Ursula was having so much fun getting
her own back on her cousins that she didn't
want to stop. But at last she decided that

they'd learnt their lesson and she let them go. They escaped through the trees, still wondering what had attacked them.

Ursula did her own little dance of glee as she watched them go. Then she quickly untied Fredbear from the totem-pole and scampered back to her tent.

Chapter Six

Ursula sat in the opening of her tent, holding a beefburger in one paw and a chip
in the other. She gobbled them down as
quickly as she could, for she knew Uncle
Andy would be coming to look for her
soon.

'RAEB A M'I, RAEB A M'I, RAEB A

M'I,' she growled softly, reciting the magic spell backwards. 'RAEB A M'I, RAEB A M'I, RAEB A M'I.'

Ursula licked her paws. Then she scrambled into her sleeping bag with Fredbear safely at her side.

She could already see a light through the trees and hear the sound of voices. She tucked the furry rug under Fredbear's chin and closed her eyes to wait for the magic to work.

When Uncle Andy shone his torch into Ursula's tent a moment later, there she was, quite herself again. She blinked in the bright light.

'Come on, Ursula,' said Uncle Andy. 'You'd better come back to the house.'

In the kitchen Ian and Jamie were drinking hot chocolate and eating shortbread biscuits and telling their mother and Aunt Prudence all about their adventure.

'I don't believe any of it,' Aunt Maggie was saying. 'I bet it's just one of your jokes.'

'It was a bear, I tell you,' Ian insisted. 'It

had great big teeth and claws and it roared and growled and snarled and bit my ankles.' He pulled his socks down to show the teethmarks, looking disappointed when he couldn't find any.

Jamie was enjoying all the drama now that the danger was over. 'It was huge,' he said, wide-eyed. 'It knocked me flat on my back. I'm not camping out there any more.'

'It sounds to me as if you both imagined it,' said Uncle Andy, shaking his head. 'There was no sign of anything when I went out. But perhaps I'd better phone the police.'

Ursula thought this had gone on long enough.

'It was me,' she said suddenly.

Everybody stared at her, open-mouthed.

Ian's face went red. 'It couldn't have

been!' he said. 'It was all brown and furry.'

Ursula tried to be as truthful as she could without giving away her secret.

'I made myself into a bear,' she told Uncle Andy. 'There's a brown furry rug in my tent. We were playing a game, and I had to rescue Fredbear from the Indians.' The two boys looked baffled when they saw that Ursula had Fredbear safely in her arms.

The grown-ups all started to laugh and the boys looked shame-faced and furious. Ursula knew they didn't understand what had really happened, but she was quite sure they wouldn't tease her again in a hurry.

Aunt Maggie poured Ursula a mug of hot chocolate. 'Well, you certainly frightened the life out of those two rascals,' she said with a smile.

Ursula looked slyly at her two cousins.

'And I'm only a girl,' she said. And she hugged Fredbear tightly in her arms.

URSULA SAILING

BY SHEILA LAVELLE
ILLUSTRATED BY THELMA LAMBERT

Ursula is an ordinary girl – with one very special secret. She can turn herself into a real, live, little bear! Sometimes this can be very useful, especially when there is a tall and difficult tree to climb. But in this new adventure for Ursula, she soon discovers that rivers and boats mean trouble for bears . . .

0 552 524484

MIDNIGHT PIRATE

BY DIANA HENDRY
ILLUSTRATED BY JANET DUCHESNE

'Oh Pirate, dear little Pirate,' whispered Ida, 'you can't stay here. The Aunts don't want a kitten.'

Nothing Ida could say would make the Aunts change their minds and it seemed as though the tiny kitten she had found under the holly bush would have to stay out in the cold and wet, unloved by anyone.

But the kitten had other ideas and even the Aunts became involved in what happened next . . .

0 552 524174

THE HAUNTING OF HEMLOCK HALL

BY LANCE SALWAY
ILLUSTRATED BY CATHIE SHUTTLEWORTH

'There's no ghosts at Hemlock Hall. Never have been and never will,' the old gardener tells Tom when he comes to work there in the holidays.

But the awful new owners, the Trotters, have other ideas. When they open the Hall to the public, they are determined that ghosts shall be among its many attractions . . .

0 552 524166

MY GANG

BY CATHERINE SEFTON
ILLUSTRATED BY CATHERINE BRADBURY

'This is my gang, Noel!' said Marty. 'It's girls only, and we're tough. We'll wallop you if you start mucking things up! Right, gang?'

Being looked after by his big sister and her gang is no joke for Noel, especially as they won't let him join. But soon Noel finds a way of making sure that he is not the only one left out . . .

0 552 524158

THE KILLER TADPOLE

BY JACQUELINE WILSON
ILLUSTRATED BY LESLEY SMITH

'Do you want to be in my gang?' Spike hissed.

Well, Spike was very good at bashing people up, so how could Nicholas refuse? But, to join the gang, he has to undergo three Terrible Ordeals.

To Nicholas's amazement, one of the Ordeals ends with a big surprise – a tadpole that keeps growing, and growing, and growing until it becomes what must be the largest tadpole in the world – the Killer Tadpole! Perhaps it can save him from Spike – and from getting bashed up!

0 552 52414X

If you would like to receive a Newsletter about our new Children's books, just fill in the coupon below with your name and address (or copy it onto a separate piece of paper if you don't want to spoil your book) and send it to:

The Children's Books Editor
Young Corgi Books
61–63 Uxbridge Road
Ealing
London W5 5SA

Please send me a Children's Newsletter:

Name: ....

Address: ....

....

....

All Children's Books are available at your bookshop or news-agent, or can be ordered from the following address:
Corgi/Bantam Books,
Cash Sales Department,
P.O. Box 11, Falmouth, Cornwall TR10 9EN

Please send a cheque or postal order (no currency) and allow 60p for postage and packing for the first book plus 25p for the second book and 15p for each additional book ordered up to a maximum charge of £1.90 in UK.

B.F.P.O. customers please allow 60p for the first book, 25p for the second book plus 15p per copy for the next 7 books, there-after 9p per book.

Overseas customers, including Eire, please allow £1.25 for postage and packing for the first book, 75p for the second book, and 28p for each subsequent title ordered.